**Aberdeenshire Library and Inform**
**www.aberdeenshire.gov.uk/**
**Renewals Hotline 01224 6**

KT-167-309

1 2 OCT 2009

HQ

1 5 NOV 2011

- 7 JUN 2014

13 NOV 2014

HQ

2 6 NOV 2010

1 3 FEB 2014

0 8 SEP 2011

HQ

0 3 AUG 2019

0 2 SEP 2015

2 2 OCT 2019

1 7 OCT 2013

HQ

1 6 SEP 2015

ABERDEENSHIRE
LIBRARIES
WITHDRAWN
FROM LIBRARY

HANSON, Dave

What now,
puss?

ALIS

2592611

First published in 2003 by
Franklin Watts
338 Euston Road
London
NW1 3BH

Franklin Watts Australia
Level 17 / 207 Kent Street
Sydney
NSW 2000

Text © Dave Hanson 2003
Illustrations © Jonathan Langley 2003

The rights of Dave Hanson to be identified as the author
and Jonathan Langley as the illustrator of this Work have
been asserted in accordance with the Copyright, Designs
and Patents Act, 1988.

All rights reserved. No part of this publication may be
reproduced, stored in a retrieval system, or transmitted
in any form or by any means, electronic, mechanical,
photocopy, recording or otherwise, without the prior
written permission of the copyright owner.

A CIP catalogue record for this book is available
from the British Library.

ISBN 978 0 7496 5365 1 (pbk)

**Series Editor:** Jackie Hamley
**Series Advisors:** Dr Barrie Wade, Dr Hilary Minns
**Design:** Peter Scoulding

Printed in China

Franklin Watts is a division of
Hachette Children's Books.

READING CORNER

# What Now, Puss?

Written by
**Dave Hanson**

Illustrated by
Jonathan Langley

**W**
FRANKLIN WATTS
LONDON•SYDNEY

### Dave Hanson

"I love climbing up mountains in summer and sliding down them in winter! I hope you enjoy the book!"

### Jonathan Langley

"I live in the Lake District with my family and Lupin the cat who is a bit like Puss!"

**ABERDEENSHIRE LIBRARY AND**
INFORMATION SERVICES

Hanson, Dave, 1

What now, puss?
/ written by
Dave Hanson /

JP                    JS

2592611              PORP

# Puss wants something.

"What do you want,
Puss? I'm working!"

7

"What do you want, Puss? I'm reading!"

"What do you want,
Puss? I'm drawing!"

11

"What do you want,
Puss? I'm playing!"

"Do you want to
go outside?"

15

# "Do you want to eat?"

"Puss! What do you want?"

19

"Do you want me?"

21

# "Come on then, Puss!"